Dear Parent:
Your child's love of reading starts here!

Every child learns to read in a different way and at his or her own speed. Some go back and forth between reading levels and read favorite books again and again. Others read through each level in order. You can help your young reader improve and become more confident by encouraging his or her own interests and abilities. From books your child reads with you to the first books he or she reads alone, there are I Can Read Books for every stage of reading:

SHARED READING
Basic language, word repetition, and whimsical illustrations, ideal for sharing with your emergent reader

BEGINNING READING
Short sentences, familiar words, and simple concepts for children eager to read on their own

READING WITH HELP
Engaging stories, longer sentences, and language play for developing readers

READING ALONE
Complex plots, challenging vocabulary, and high-interest topics for the independent reader

ADVANCED READING
Short paragraphs, chapters, and exciting themes for the perfect bridge to chapter books

I Can Read Books have introduced children to the joy of reading since 1957. Featuring award-winning authors and illustrators and a fabulous cast of beloved characters, I Can Read Books set the standard for beginning readers.

A lifetime of discovery begins with the magical words "I Can Read!"

Visit www.icanread.com for information on enriching your child's reading experience.

The Early Adventures of
Amelia Bedelia

by Herman Parish ✿ pictures by Lynne Avril

I Can Read!™

The Early Adventures of Amelia Bedelia

by Herman Parish ❋ pictures by Lynne Avril

HARPER
An Imprint of HarperCollinsPublishers

Table of Contents

Amelia Bedelia

·Makes a Friend·

by Herman Parish ✹ pictures by Lynne Avril

Amelia Bedelia was lucky.

Her best friend lived next door.

"Hello, Jen!" said Amelia Bedelia.

"Hi, Amelia Bedelia!" said Jen.

11

Amelia Bedelia and Jen

had been friends

since they were babies.

They baked together.

SALE !!!
Fresh. Mud
PIES

They dressed up together.

They played music together.

Amelia Bedelia even showed Jen
how to bowl.

"They play so well together,"
said Amelia Bedelia's mother.
"They sure do," said Jen's mother.
"Even though they are
as different as night and day."

Then one day,
Jen and her parents
moved away.
Amelia Bedelia and her parents
were very sad.

Amelia Bedelia missed Jen.

She missed Jen every day.

She wished Jen would come back.

One morning, a moving van pulled up.

"Did Jen come back?"

asked Amelia Bedelia.

"I don't think so,"
said Amelia Bedelia's mother.
"We must have new neighbors."

Amelia Bedelia's mother
watched the movers.
"Oh, look," she said.
"I see a fancy footstool."

Amelia Bedelia did not look.
She wanted Jen back.

"Look!" said Amelia Bedelia's mother.

"I see a coffee table."

Amelia Bedelia still did not look.

She just kept drawing.

Amelia Bedelia's
mother said,
"I see some
big armchairs."

"I see a loveseat."

"I see a twin bed."

Finally, Amelia Bedelia looked
at Jen's old house.
Then she looked at her drawings.
"Our new neighbors sound strange,"
she said.

That night, Amelia Bedelia
told her dad
about the new neighbors.

He loved her pictures.

"Amazing!" her dad said.

"I hope they have a pool table."

The next morning,
Amelia Bedelia and her mother
baked blueberry muffins.

They took the muffins
next door.

A lady opened the door.

"Hello there," she said.

"My name is Mrs. Adams.

You must be my new neighbors."

27

"No," said Amelia Bedelia.

"We already live here.

You are my new neighbor."

"You know," said Mrs. Adams,
"I think both of us are right.
Do come in."

"Mmmm," Mrs. Adams said.

"What smells so good?"

"My mom does," said Amelia Bedelia.

"I don't wear perfume yet."

Jen's house looked different.

Every room was full of boxes.

"Welcome to my mess,"

said Mrs. Adams.

"I will live out of boxes for a while."

That sounded fun to Amelia Bedelia.

"Are the twins in their bed?"

asked Amelia Bedelia.

"My goodness," said Mrs. Adams.

"You have sharp eyes."

Amelia Bedelia hoped that was good.

"My twin grandchildren

will visit today," said Mrs. Adams.

"Their names are Mary and Marty."

The twins visited that afternoon.
"Our grandma is a lot of fun,"
they told Amelia Bedelia.

They were right!
It was great to have a friend
right next door again.

Amelia Bedelia and Mrs. Adams
baked together.

They dressed up together.

They played music together.

"They have so much fun together,"
said Amelia Bedelia's father.
"They sure do,"
said Amelia Bedelia's mother.
"Even though they are
as different as night and day."

One day Jen came back to visit.

Mrs. Adams took both girls

to a real bowling alley.

"This is the best day ever,"
said Amelia Bedelia.
"I have a best old friend
and a best new friend.
We are three best friends together!"

Amelia Bedelia
• Sleeps Over •

by **Herman Parish** ✸ pictures by **Lynne Avril**

Amelia Bedelia was excited.

Tonight was her very first sleepover.

All the girls in her class

were going to Rose's house

for a slumber party.

41

Amelia Bedelia and her mother

drove to Rose's house.

"Is a slumber party fun?"

asked Amelia Bedelia.

"Because sleeping is boring."

"You might not sleep much,"

said her mother.

"You will play, eat pizza, paint nails . . ."

"Do we paint the nails
and then hammer them?"
asked Amelia Bedelia.

"Or do we hammer them first?"

Amelia Bedelia's mother laughed.

"You'll have fun, sweetie," she said.

"I promise."

When Amelia Bedelia arrived,
the front door swung open.
Her friends ran out to greet her.
Rose's mother came outside, too.

45

"Good luck," said Amelia Bedelia's mom.

"I think I'll need it!" said Rose's mother.

"I am a light sleeper."

"Me too," said Amelia Bedelia.

She reached into her backpack

and pulled out her flashlight.

"I sleep with this light every night."

The girls played board games.

Amelia Bedelia had worried

that she would be bored,

but she was not.

Next, everyone went outside
and played tag
until the sun began to set.

"The pizza is here!"
called Rose's father.
"Come and get it!"

"And for dessert," said Rose's mother,
"we will toast marshmallows
and make s'mores."

"Won't that wreck your toaster?"
asked Amelia Bedelia.

"Marshmallows melt into gooey, blobby . . ."

Rose's father laughed.

"We'll toast them on the grill," he said.

After the pizza was gone,

Dawn speared a marshmallow

on Amelia Bedelia's stick.

Holly showed her how to turn it

carefully and slowly

to get a crunchy brown skin.

Amelia Bedelia put her marshmallow

on top of a chocolate bar

between two graham crackers.

"Yum!" said Amelia Bedelia.

"I'd like some more, please!"

"Now you know why

they're called s'mores!" said Rose.

After many more s'mores,

the girls went inside the house.

They put on their pajamas,

but it was not time to slumber yet.

Rose brought out bottles

of glittery nail polish

in more colors than the rainbow.

Every color had the perfect name.

She saved her left foot for "Cotton Candy Cupcake."

Amelia Bedelia sighed and said,
"I'm so happy
we don't have to hammer them!"

Too soon, the clock struck ten.

"Bedtime, girls!" said Rose's mother.

"Lights out, and no giggling allowed!"

Oh well, thought Amelia Bedelia.

Here comes the slumber part

of this slumber party.

Off went the lights and lamps.

On went Amelia Bedelia's flashlight.

She showed her friends how to make

shadow puppets on the wall.

59

One by one,

the girls fell asleep.

All except Amelia Bedelia.

She was not one bit sleepy.

She made a rabbit.

60

Then a barking dog.

Then an elephant

with a trunk to grab . . .

Oops!

Her flashlight went out.

"Oh, no," said Amelia Bedelia.

What light would keep her company now?

Then Amelia Bedelia noticed

a very bright light

peeking into the family room.

She pulled back the curtains.

A full moon shone down on her.

Now there was too much light!

Amelia Bedelia dragged her sleeping bag
under Rose's Ping-Pong table.

Perfect, thought Amelia Bedelia.
Now I am having a sleepover
and a sleep under.

Amelia Bedelia snuggled down
into her cozy sleeping bag.
She gazed up at the moon.
She had heard people say that
there was a man in the moon.
She'd never seen him, until tonight.

He looked just like her dad.

Amelia Bedelia closed her eyes.

A second later, she was sound asleep.

The next morning,

the girls had a pillow fight.

Then they made chocolate chip pancakes

and helped to clean up the mess.

Amelia Bedelia's dad picked her up.

"Nice nails," said her father.

"Thanks, moon man," said Amelia Bedelia.

"Huh?" said her father.

"You sound like you need to take a nap."

And so Amelia Bedelia did,

all the way home.

Amelia Bedelia
·Hits the Trail·

by Herman Parish ✻ pictures by Lynne Avril

Amelia Bedelia was going hiking.

Her entire class was going, too.

"Let's hit the trail," said Miss Edwards,

Amelia Bedelia's teacher.

The trail was steep.

Everyone stepped over a big tree root.

Amelia Bedelia was chatting

and looking up at the birds and . . .

SPLAT!!

Amelia Bedelia fell flat on her face.

"Are you okay?" asked Miss Edwards.

"I'm okay," said Amelia Bedelia.

"But the next time I hit the trail,

I'll use this stick instead of my face!"

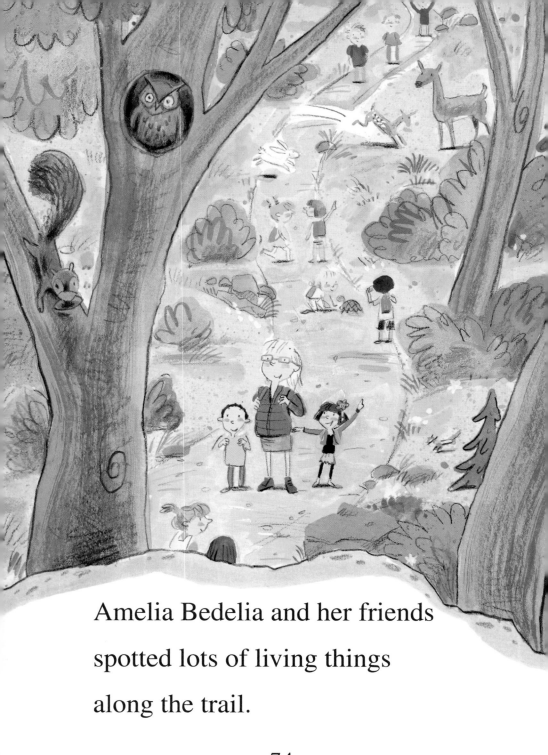

Amelia Bedelia and her friends
spotted lots of living things
along the trail.

They saw a deer
and a rabbit.

They saw squirrels
and chipmunks.

They saw insects
crawling along the ground

and flying in the air.

Birds chirped
in the trees.

When a snake crossed the trail,
Chip let out a yell.

"Relax," said Penny.
"It is more scared of you
than you are of it."

The class walked slowly.

"Let's move a little faster,"

said Miss Edwards.

"Pick up your snail's pace."

Amelia Bedelia looked for a snail

with a pace to pick up.

Maybe she could find one

for the classroom nature table.

77

"I'm hungry," said Clay.

"Can we eat lunch?"

Miss Edwards read her map.

"There is a stream ahead," she said.

"We can stop there for a bite."

"I have lots of bites," said Amelia Bedelia.

"I can see water!" said Penny.

The class raced to the stream.

80

"We'll eat lunch on the bank.

Dig in!" said Miss Edwards.

Amelia Bedelia
didn't see a bank,

or even a cash machine.

Was there treasure buried here?
Why else would Miss Edwards tell them
to dig in?

82

It was time to go back to school.

Wade was the last to finish his lunch.

"Let's go, Wade," said Miss Edwards.

"Yay!" said Amelia Bedelia.

Amelia Bedelia took off
her shoes and socks
and waded right into the stream.

Soon everyone was splashing

with Amelia Bedelia.

Even Miss Edwards joined the fun.

As they walked back,
everyone found things
for the nature table.

Daisy picked a daisy.

Holly plucked
a sprig of holly.

Rose found
a wild rose.

Amelia Bedelia
picked up fallen leaves.

"What did you find, Amelia Bedelia?"
asked Miss Edwards.

"These are my leafs," said Amelia Bedelia.

Miss Edwards smiled.

"When you have more than one leaf,
you say *leaves*," she said.

That made sense to Amelia Bedelia.

In the fall, every leaf

had to leave its tree.

Amelia Bedelia knew

she would not think anymore

of a leaf falling off a tree.

She would think

it was leaving

its tree.

"Nice leaves," said Skip.

"You have maple,

oak,

and chestnut," he said.

Skip knew a lot about trees.

"What is this red one?"

asked Amelia Bedelia.

"Uh-oh," said Skip. "That is poison ivy!"

YEE-AHHHH!!

Amelia Bedelia threw the leaves

up in the air.

Her leaves were leaving again!

Skip laughed so hard

he fell on the ground.

"I was joking!" he said.

Amelia Bedelia was not laughing.

"That was a mean trick," she said.

"Maybe you should take a hike,"
said Skip.

"I am," said Amelia Bedelia.

"And now I don't have anything
for the nature table."

93

Amelia Bedelia's lip trembled.

"I'm sorry, Amelia Bedelia," said Skip.

He helped Amelia Bedelia

pick up her leaves.

"Hold still!" Skip said.

"Are you teasing again?"

asked Amelia Bedelia.

"No. You have a hitchhiker," said Skip.

He pointed at a caterpillar.

The caterpillar was crawling

on Amelia Bedelia's backpack.

"Wow!" said Amelia Bedelia.

Amelia Bedelia's caterpillar

was the star of the nature table.

Then it was the star

of Amelia Bedelia's classroom . . .

96

until it hit the trail.

Amelia Bedelia
·Tries Her Luck·

by Herman Parish ✹ pictures by Lynne Avril

Amelia Bedelia was getting ready

to go to school when . . .

CRASH!

"I'm sorry!" said Amelia Bedelia.

"Accidents happen, sweetie,"

said her mother.

"The important thing

is that you are not hurt."

At school, Amelia Bedelia told her friends about the accident.

"You're in trouble," said Clay.
"Breaking a mirror means
seven years of bad luck."

"Seven years!"
said Amelia Bedelia.
"That's almost my whole life!"

"Even worse," said Rose.

"Today is Friday the thirteenth.

Bad luck gets doubled today."

"That's fourteen years!"

said Amelia Bedelia.

"I'll have bad luck forever!"

"Amelia Bedelia," said Joy,

"you can change your luck."

"That's right," said Heather.

"My dad always says,

See a penny, pick it up,

all the day you'll have good luck."

Amelia Bedelia picked up Penny.

"Put me down!" said Penny.

"Heather means a penny coin,

not a Penny person."

At recess, the whole class
tried to help Amelia Bedelia
change her luck.

They searched
for a four-leaf clover.

They looked for
a lucky horseshoe.

They tried to find a rabbit's foot.

The playground didn't have any of
those things.

"I'm sorry, Amelia Bedelia," said Clay.
"We struck out. You are out of luck."

Amelia Bedelia made a plan.

If she could not find luck,

she would make her own luck.

Two Rabbit's Feet =
Double Luck

12 Leaf Clover =
3 x
Luck

ur Horseshoes =
4 x Luck

111

Amelia Bedelia's teacher, Miss Edwards,

saw her drawings.

She also saw that Amelia Bedelia was upset.

"Are you all right?" asked Miss Edwards.

"No, I am all wrong,"
said Amelia Bedelia.
She told Miss Edwards
about breaking the mirror
and her double bad luck.

"Amelia Bedelia," said Miss Edwards,
"today is my lucky day.
Friday the thirteenth
is the perfect day
to talk about luck."

The class listed lucky and unlucky things.

They talked about bad luck and good luck.

There were all kinds of questions.

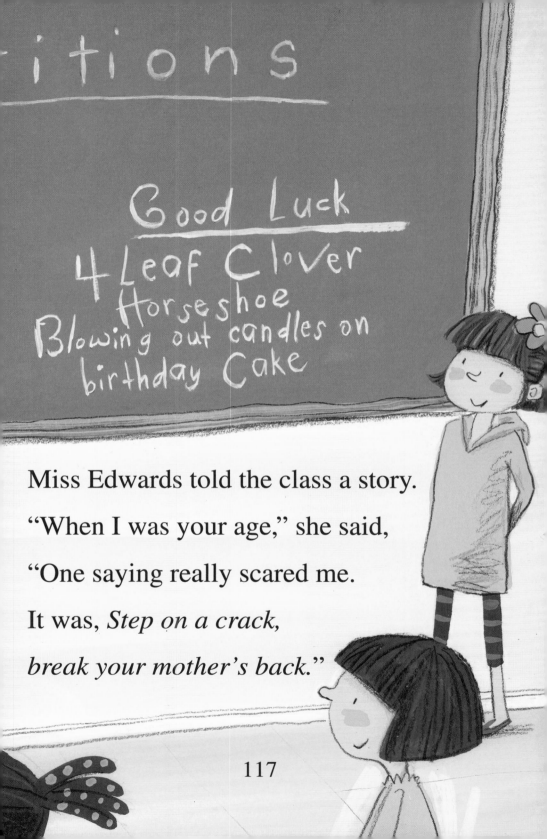

...itions

Good Luck

4 Leaf Clover
Horseshoe
Blowing out candles on
birthday Cake

Miss Edwards told the class a story.

"When I was your age," she said,

"One saying really scared me.

It was, *Step on a crack,*

break your mother's back."

117

"That's terrible," said Amelia Bedelia.

"But it isn't true," said Miss Edwards.

"Just like breaking a mirror isn't bad luck."

"Breaking a mirror is bad luck," said Clay.

"It's bad luck for the mirror!"

Everyone laughed.

Amelia Bedelia laughed hardest of all.

She felt a lot better.

As Amelia Bedelia was walking home,
she saw a crack in the sidewalk.
"Bad luck? Ha!" she said.

She stepped on the crack.
She stepped on every crack she saw.
When she spied the biggest one of all,
Amelia Bedelia stomped on it.

Then Amelia Bedelia turned onto her street,
and she stopped in her tracks.

There was an ambulance

in front of her house.

Amelia Bedelia raced home.

Breaking the mirror was an accident,

but she had stepped on those cracks

on purpose.

"Mom!" yelled Amelia Bedelia.

"I didn't mean to break your back!"

The ambulance was pulling away.

"Mom!" cried Amelia Bedelia. "Mom!"

"Amelia Bedelia!" said her mother.

"I'm with Mrs. Adams, sweetie."

Amelia Bedelia whirled around.

Her mom was with their neighbor.

Her back was fine!

Amelia Bedelia ran to her mom.

She gave her the biggest,

longest, strongest hug ever.

"Ouch, honey!"

said Amelia Bedelia's mother.

"Do you want to break my back?"

"No, never!" said Amelia Bedelia.

"You just missed the excitement,"
said Mrs. Adams.

"I got a ride home in an ambulance
after my checkup."

"Are you okay?" asked Amelia Bedelia.

"I am fine," said Mrs. Adams.

"Knock on wood."

Then Mrs. Adams knocked three times
on her porch railing.

Tomorrow, Amelia Bedelia would add
"knock on wood" to the list
her class had made.
Today, worrying about luck
had worn her out.

Amelia Bedelia thought about

her family and her great friends.

She thought that the mirror

Mrs. Adams gave her was cool.

Amelia Bedelia felt like she was

the luckiest person in the world.

Amelia Bedelia
· Joins the Club ·

by Herman Parish ❋ pictures by Lynne Avril

Amelia Bedelia loved her school.

She liked the way everyone got along.

They worked together.

They played together.

They took turns and shared everything.

131

"Let Pat have a turn."

"Daisy gets the glue next."

"You can go
ahead of me."

"I like your idea better."

132

"This way is easier."

"Try some of my chips."

Amelia Bedelia's class

always got along . . . until it rained.

That was when her class split in two.

134

"We are the Puddle Stompers!"

Puddle Jumpers took running leaps
and flew over puddles.

Puddle Stompers took running leaps and landed in puddles.

"Come sail over puddles with us,"
said Clay.

"Puddles are not big enough
to sail across," said Amelia Bedelia.

"Come dive into puddles with us,"
said Holly.

"Puddles are too small to dive into,"
said Amelia Bedelia.

Both clubs wanted Amelia Bedelia.

Jumping and stomping looked like fun.

She liked every Jumper and Stomper.

But if she picked one club

she might hurt the feelings

of her friends in the other club.

Amelia Bedelia asked her teacher for help.

"It sounds like you are torn

between two choices," said Miss Edwards.

"You are right," said Amelia Bedelia.

"And it really hurts!"

After school,

the Stompers and the Jumpers

tried to make Amelia Bedelia

choose one club or the other.

"I'll decide at recess tomorrow,"

Amelia Bedelia told them.

Amelia Bedelia's mother
was waiting for her at the bus stop.
"Rain, rain, go away.
Come again another day!"
said her mother.

"Not another day," said Amelia Bedelia.

"Rain and puddles, don't come here.

Come again another year!"

"Sorry, sweetie," said her mother.

"It is going to rain buckets tonight."

Amelia Bedelia was worried.

Buckets of rain tonight meant

millions of puddles tomorrow!

At supper, Amelia Bedelia told her parents

about being caught between the two clubs.

"Wow!" said her father.

"You are in a club sandwich."

Amelia Bedelia knew her dad was joking,

but at least he knew how she felt.

"Why choose?" asked her mother.

"Can't you join two clubs?"

Amelia Bedelia stopped chewing.

That was the answer!

She hugged her mom.

At last she knew just what to do.

The next day, it stopped raining
right before recess.
The playground was filled
with oodles of puddles.

150

Jumpers and Stompers rushed outside.

Everyone wanted to hear which club

Amelia Bedelia was going to join.

"I am joining my own club!"

said Amelia Bedelia.

"It is called the Hop, Skip, and Jump club."

Then she showed them what to do.

First she hopped over a puddle.

"Hooray!" said the Jumpers.

Then Amelia Bedelia skipped

to another puddle

and jumped into it with a splash.

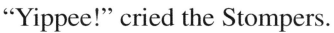
"Yippee!" cried the Stompers.

Every one of the Jumpers and Stompers

wanted to be in the

Hop, Skip, and Jump club.

Even Miss Edwards!

"Nice work, Amelia Bedelia,"
said Miss Edwards.
"By joining your own club,
you joined the other two clubs together."

Amelia Bedelia was not

thinking about that.

She was just happy to see her class

getting along again, even in the rain.